Whose Mess Is This?

By Carol Roth
Illustrated by Richard Walz

A GOLDEN BOOK • NEW YORK
Western Publishing Company, Inc., Racine, Wisconsin 53404

Betsy and Bonnie were sisters. They looked alike, but in many ways they were as different as night and day.

For one thing, Betsy was messy and Bonnie was neat. That sometimes made it difficult for them to share the same room.

Bonnie hated her sister's messy habits.
One day she said, "You know, our room doesn't have to look like a pigpen. And you don't have to look so messy! Your hair isn't combed. Your face isn't washed. You look like a pig!"

"But I am a pig," said Betsy. "I like me this way."

"Well, I don't," said Bonnie. "You should be neater, just like me."

"I don't want to be like you!" shouted Betsy.
The two sisters argued and argued. Their voices
got louder and louder.

When their mother heard them yelling, she said,
"I will put an end to all this arguing."

She took a piece of chalk and drew a line right
down the middle of their room.

"Now there are two sides," she said. "Each of you
can keep your side any way you want."

The sisters thought that was a great idea, but soon they had new problems.

Betsy couldn't use Bonnie's desk to do her jigsaw puzzle. Bonnie could hardly see the TV because it was on Betsy's side.

"This is no fun," said Bonnie. "I'm going out to play."

"Ha, ha, you can't," said Betsy. "The door is on my side."

"So what," said Bonnie. "The window is on my side."

Bonnie walked over to the window. Without looking very carefully, she jumped right out. She landed in a big mud puddle.

"Oh, no!" she cried. "My clothes are all dirty. My hair is dirty, too. I'm a mess!"

But then she noticed that the mud felt soft and warm. Bonnie began to enjoy herself. She made mud balls and mud pies. She was having so much fun that she forgot all about being messy.

Meanwhile, Betsy began to wonder what Bonnie was doing outside. She went over to the window to see.

As she crossed over the line she noticed something.
Bonnie's side of the room looked larger than hers.
Was it really bigger? Or did it just look bigger
because it was neat? Betsy wondered.

"Look at all this space. If I picked up my things, I would have lots of room, too. I would have a place to do my puzzles. I would have a place to color and draw.

"I would even have a place to practice my ballet,"
she thought.

She couldn't wait to tell Bonnie that now she liked
the idea of having a tidy room.

Betsy looked out the window. She saw Bonnie
playing in the mud and burst out laughing.
"Just look at you!" she said. "You are a mess!"

"Come play with me," said Bonnie. "This is fun."
"I will, in a minute," said Betsy. "There is something I have to do first."

Betsy cleaned up her side of the room. Bonnie
would certainly be surprised, Betsy thought.

Then she went outside to play with Bonnie. The
two sisters made mud balls and mud pies until it
was time to wash up for supper.

After that day, Betsy and Bonnie decided they didn't really need a line drawn down the middle of their room. Bonnie said it was okay to be messy once in a while. Betsy said she would try to be neat—at least some of the time. And sometimes their room was messy and sometimes it was neat, but from that day on, the two sisters found that sharing a room could be twice as nice.